Fic   2.0
Fra

T 63886

D1131946

DISCARD

$12⁴⁵

7-04

Follett

COLUMBINE SCHOOL
Fort Morgan, CO

The Jayhawk Horse Mystery

(A Cody Smith Mystery)

by Dorothy Francis

Perfection Learning®

Cover and Inside Illustrations: William Ersland

About the Author

Dorothy Francis has written many books and stories for children and adults.

Ms. Francis holds a bachelor of music degree from the University of Kansas. She has traveled with an all-girl dance band, taught music in public and private schools, and served as a correspondence teacher for the Institute of Children's Literature in Connecticut.

She and her husband, Richard, divide their time between Marshalltown, Iowa, and Big Pine Key, Florida.

Text © 2001 by Perfection Learning® Corporation.

All rights reserved. No part of this book may be used or reproduced in any manner whatsoever without written permission from the publisher.

Printed in the United States of America. For information, contact

Perfection Learning® Corporation

1000 North Second Avenue, P.O. Box 500

Logan, Iowa 51546-0500

Phone: 800-831-4190 • Fax: 712-644-2392

Paperback ISBN 0-7891-5349-1

Cover Craft® ISBN 0-7807-9728-0

Printed in the U.S.A.

Table of Contents

1

A Mystery to Solve

My name is Cody Smith. Mom and I live in Cottonwood, Kansas. We're new here.

Sometimes jobs were hard to find. We had to move wherever Mom could find a job. Here in Cottonwood, Mom worked as a store detective in an outlet mall.

THE JAYHAWK HORSE MYSTERY

"Someone's moved my secret journal," Maria called.

"It's right where you left it," I called back.

Maria Romero lived with us too. Her parents were working in Italy. It was supposed to be just for the summer. But the job was taking longer than expected. So Maria was staying with us until they finished.

I liked having Maria around. And her parents paid Mom to look after her. So it was a good arrangement.

Maria was lucky. Her parents would return when their job ended. Last year, my dad walked out on us. He won't be coming back.

I missed him. And I felt sorry for him too. He lost a great family.

Maria wanted to be a writer someday. She kept ideas in a secret journal. She planned to write them into stories.

Sometimes I tried to peek at her journal. She used to write weird article ideas and riddles. Now most of her ideas were strange questions. I didn't know the answers. Neither did she.

"Cody? Maria?" Mom called. "Breakfast."

My feet hit the floor. I beat Maria into the bathroom. Good! She took forever to comb her dark curls.

My hair was red and stubby. I combed it with the washcloth. That saved time. But Maria's hair looked prettier.

A Mystery to Solve

"I smell pancakes and maple syrup," I called to Maria. I liked good smells in my lungs. I breathed deeply and hurried to the kitchen.

"Save me some," Maria called back.

Our house was handkerchief small. But we liked it. It was cozy and comfortable. And it had a name—*Linden House*. Those words were painted above the front door.

Most of the trees on our street were cottonwoods. But the big one in our yard was a linden. That's where *Linden House* got its name.

Mom was already in disguise for work. She was wearing a curly blond wig and a black shirt. Her yellow pants were like balloons gathered at her ankles.

"Won't people remember that outfit?" I asked. "You'll blow your cover."

"Not so," Mom said. "There's a circus in town. I'll fit in with the mall crowd. And I'll wear a different disguise each day."

"When I grow up, I want to be a detective too," I said. "A famous detective."

Once I thought Dad might return if I became famous. Then I got my name in the paper last summer. And Dad didn't even call. Now I still wanted to be famous—but not for Dad's sake.

I wanted to do good things for the world. I wanted to make a difference. And I was working on it every day.

Solving mysteries was one way I made a difference. Maria helped me. We were pretty good at it too.

In New York, we solved the Bigfoot mystery. In Iowa, we solved the missing-emerald mystery. In Florida, we almost caught a kidnapper. But so far I wasn't famous.

I was working on being an eponym. That was a person who did something memorable. And then his name became a household word.

Harry Houdini was an example. He was a famous escape artist. Now people said "He's a regular Houdini." That meant the person was good at getting out of tricky situations.

"He's a famous Cody Smith." That's what I wanted people to say. It would mean the person was a great detective like me.

But the eponym thing might fail. So I had backup plans.

I hadn't told anyone yet. But I wanted my picture on a postage stamp. That would mean real fame.

"Lots of famous people came from Kansas," Maria said. She sat down at the breakfast table. Sometimes Maria read my mind.

"Maybe some Kansas fame will rub off on me," I said. "Dwight Eisenhower came from Kansas. He became president."

"I might write about Amelia Earhart," Maria said.

"She was a famous pilot. Or maybe I'll write about Anna Barkman."

In English class, we had to choose a famous Kansan to study. Then we had to write a paper about that person.

"I've never heard of Anna Barkman," I said.

"She was a Russian Mennonite girl. The Mennonites moved to Kansas for religious freedom."

"When?" I asked.

"Many years ago," Maria said. "Anna was eight. Her job was to pack her family's wheat seed. She gathered two gallons of seed. Mennonites called it *Turkey Red.*"

"What a strange name," I said.

"Kansans had never seen such wonderful seed. Turkey-Red seed improved wheat growing in Kansas. Anna's story made Kansas history books."

"Cool!" I said. "If an eight-year-old girl can win fame, so can I."

I noticed Maria's headphones lying near her plate.

"What were you listening to?" I asked.

"Rock," she said. Rock was Maria's favorite kind of music.

"My favorite rock group is Mount Rushmore," I said. That was an old joke. Maria didn't laugh.

She unwrapped a cinnamon ball and laid it beside her plate.

"Pancakes first," she said. "Then a cinnamon ball. Want one?"

I shook my head. Cinnamon balls burned my mouth. It was too early in the morning for that. But I was glad Maria ate them. They gave her a great smell.

"Have you found a current event for today?" Maria asked.

"No," I said. "I'll find one after breakfast." Miss Reeding, one of our teachers, liked current events. She wanted us to read the newspaper every day. I liked that. Sometimes I found mysteries to think about.

"Current events give me story ideas," Maria said.

"Better eat," Mom said. "It's getting late."

After breakfast I grabbed the *Cottonwood Gazette.* Maria grabbed the *Kansas City Star.* We looked for current events.

"I've got one!" Maria shouted. She usually beat me.

"What's it about?" I asked.

"It's about an American tourist," she said. "He blocked traffic for miles on the London Bridge. He drove on the right-hand side of the street. In England, they drive on the left-hand side."

"That's cool," I admitted. Sometimes Maria bugged me. She always found cool stuff. But today I topped her.

"Look at this, Maria." I pointed. "This woman,

LaMer, thought she bought an antique carousel horse. But it was a fake. Cops are hunting for the crook that cheated her."

"LaMer who?" Maria asked. "What's her last name?"

"The article doesn't say," I said. "Maybe she's so famous she just goes by one name."

I thought about that. Awesome! Maybe someday I'd be that famous. People would just say *Cody*. And everyone would know they meant *Cody Smith*.

"Cody, look!" Maria read over my shoulder. "LaMer lives on our street. Her house is on the next block."

"Double awesome," I said. "Maybe we could meet her. This may be a mystery for us to solve."

"Maybe so," Maria agreed.

I clipped the articles. Then Maria put them in our current-events folders. We shoved our folders into our backpacks and headed for school.

Cottonwood trees formed a leafy tunnel over the sidewalk. The September air smelled fresh and clean. It held a morning coolness that I liked. By afternoon we'd be sweltering. That was Kansas for you.

We reached LaMer's address. We slowed down. Two police cars were parked in front.

Maria dropped a cinnamon ball on purpose. That gave us an excuse to stop and search. That way we could study the mystery situation.

"There she is," Maria whispered. "Look—in the doorway."

I gulped. LaMer stood at least six feet tall. She scowled. She looked like an owl watching for field mice.

I found Maria's cinnamon ball and unwrapped it. I popped it into my mouth without thinking. My tongue burned. My eyes began to water.

I liked to nickname people. But I couldn't think of a nickname for LaMer. Besides, she already had a unique name.

The policemen were watching us. I saw them through my watering eyes. I shivered. But I wouldn't admit my fear to Maria.

I wanted to run to school. But I also wanted to hear what LaMer was telling the policemen.

2

The Contest

It wasn't polite to eavesdrop. People weren't happy when you listened in on their conversations. But detectives did it a lot. It was their business. How else would they learn secret stuff?

But the policemen didn't like us eavesdropping on them. One of them scowled at us.

Maria smiled at him. "Good morning," Maria said.

"Good morning," the policeman replied. He smiled back.

Maria was a peacemaker. She could usually smooth over a bad situation. Mom said I should take lessons from her.

We jogged on to school. Our school looked like a lot of schools. It was made of red brick. It had two stories and lots of windows.

One thing was different, though. It had giant sunflowers growing at the doorway. They almost reached the second-floor windows. Blackbirds perched on the sunflowers and ate the seeds.

There was a gold-lettered sign above the doorway. It read CHISHOLM TRAIL MIDDLE SCHOOL.

"Do you know what the school is named for?" Maria asked me as we approached the entrance.

"It was named after Jesse Chisholm," I said. "I saw an article about him inside. It's behind glass on a bulletin board."

"What did he do?" Maria asked.

"Years ago, he blazed a wilderness trail," I said. "Cattlemen used it. They drove cattle from Texas to sell in Kansas."

"There's Miss Reeding," Maria said. "I like her a lot. Today's her red day."

We both waved to our teacher. I seldom nicknamed classroom teachers. It wasn't a good plan.

14

"Her red day?" I asked.

"Haven't you noticed?" Maria asked. "She always wears a denim jumper. And she has a different color for each day. Monday is red. Tuesday is yellow. Wednesday . . ."

I sighed. Clothes were a girl thing. I noticed different stuff—more important stuff.

Miss Reeding was short. She was young like Mom. Her hair was orange as a carrot. And she usually smiled.

"There's the bell," Maria said. "Let's go."

Maria joined the jam at the school door. I waited until the crowd thinned. I hated it when everyone tried to breathe the same air.

I smelled fresh paint and chalk dust. I liked those school smells.

And I liked our English classroom. Miss Reeding thumbtacked book jackets to our bulletin board. It made me want to read those books.

We did a lot of foot shuffling. But at last we settled into our seats. Miss Reeding collected lunch money.

Then she checked the roll. But she no longer called our names. She knew us all by now. She just looked around to see if anyone was missing.

Miss Reeding was our homeroom and English teacher. I wished she were our all-day teacher. But all-day teachers were for little kids. Middle graders moved from class to class.

"All right," Miss Reeding said. "Time for current events. Who'll be first?"

One boy told us about a new building at Haskell University. That's an important Kansas college for Native American kids.

A girl told us about Kansas City fountains. People called Kansas City the *City of Fountains*. It was about 60 miles from Cottonwood.

Then Maria told about the traffic jam at London Bridge.

"Why don't they drive on the right?" one boy asked. "That's the best way."

"There's no best way," Miss Reeding said. "Londoners may wonder why we don't drive on the left. We need to consider differing points of view. Cody, you're next."

I told about LaMer and the carousel horse. Some kids called it a merry-go-round horse. It was the same thing. But I thought *carousel* sounded more important.

"I'd like to solve that mystery," I said.

"What's LaMer's last name?" a girl asked.

"LaMer Holcomb," Miss Reeding said. "Everyone in Cottonwood knows her. She's a well-known artist. *LaMer* means 'the sea.' She's named for the Kansas Sea."

"The Kansas *Sea*?" someone called out. "There's no sea in Kansas."

"There used to be," Miss Reeding said. "Millions of years ago, the Chalk Ocean covered Kansas."

"How do you know?" another voice called.

Miss Reeding smiled. "Scientists have proven it. They found seashell fossils in Kansas. And they've found mosasaur skeletons."

"Where are the fossils now?" Maria asked.

"Many of them are in university museums," Miss Reeding said. "Someday we might take a field trip to see them."

I wanted to talk more about a field trip. I liked field trips. But Maria spoke up.

"Why's an antique carousel horse so valuable?" she asked.

"Old things have value," Miss Reeding explained. "And so do rare things. Items a hundred years old or older are called *antiques*."

"What if an old thing is less than a hundred years old?" I asked.

"If it's interesting, it's called a *collectible*," Miss Reeding explained. "LaMer collects carousel horses. Some are antiques. Others are just collectibles."

"Have you seen them?" Maria asked.

"Yes," Miss Reeding said. "She's told me a lot about them too. The carousel idea started in medieval times. The horses were mounted on wood beams. They circled a pole."

"Did the knights ride them?" someone asked.

"Did they carry swords?" someone else shouted out.

"Yes," Miss Reeding said. "Knights-in-training rode the wooden horses. They practiced thrusting. They aimed their lances at hanging brass rings. Medieval teachers called that setup a *carousel*."

"We still see carousels at fairs," I said. "Electricity and computers make them move. But what made those antique carousels move?"

"At first, men or horses pulled them," Miss Reeding said. "Later, power from steam engines and electricity turned them. They had many names—*Roundabouts*, *Flying Jennies*, *Spinning Jennies*."

"I've seen merry-go-rounds that had other animals," Maria said.

"Right," Miss Reeding said. "Some have lions, chickens, camels—whatever."

"What kind of animals does LaMer collect?" a student in the front row asked.

"LaMer likes the antique carousel horses. They're very valuable," Miss Reeding explained. "It's too bad that someone cheated her."

"Maybe I can find that crook," I said.

Miss Reeding frowned. "I know you want to help, Cody. But be careful. Confronting a crook is dangerous. Better leave it to the police."

The Contest

"Do you think I could talk to LaMer?" I asked.

Miss Reeding started to answer. But a voice from the intercom on the wall stopped her. The booming voice came from our principal, Mr. Sampson.

I'd nicknamed him *Wall Voice*. His voice was loud and forceful over the intercom. Sometimes the walls seemed to shake when he spoke.

But his body didn't match his voice. He was short and slim. His dark brown hair was highlighted with shades of gray. His blue eyes could be kind. But often they were serious and stern. He reminded me of a coiled spring—tense and ready for action.

"Students," Wall Voice began. "I'm announcing a SPECIAL CONTEST."

Wall Voice often talked in uppercase.

"The contest is open to EACH OF YOU. We need a new anti-drug slogan. TEN WORDS OR LESS. *Say no to drugs* has been overused. Show me something NEW—something DIFFERENT.

"I'm offering a prize. It will be a field trip for the winner's classroom. The class will get to choose where they'd like to go. And I'll print the winning slogan on poster board. I'll make a poster for each classroom.

"The deadline is A WEEK FROM TODAY," Wall Voice continued. "SHOW ME WHAT YOU CAN DO."

What a day! Maria and I had a mystery to solve.

19

And we had a contest to enter. I could hardly wait until school was out that afternoon.

Maybe the police could use some help with LaMer's crook. Crooks could be hard to capture.

I also wanted to talk to LaMer. Then I remembered her scary owl look. Maybe she didn't like kids. What if she wouldn't talk to us?

3

Meet LaMer

Maria and I walked slowly to LaMer's house. We didn't want to attract attention.

"What a strange house," Maria said.

"The back part looks like a log cabin," I said. "But the front's an ordinary house. Let's knock on the door."

"That's what visitors usually do." Maria removed her headphones. We knocked. But nobody answered.

"Maybe she's in the log-cabin part," I said. "Let's try the back door."

We walked around the side of the house. We passed several windows. I couldn't resist looking in.

"What are those strange things on the walls?" I asked.

"The room's too shadowy," Maria said. "I can't tell."

"Look at the messy floor," I said. "There's sawdust everywhere. And lots of wood shavings in the sawdust."

A low voice spoke behind us. We both jumped.

"What are you kids doing? You're trespassing on private property."

We whirled around. I looked up and up and up. At last my eyes met LaMer's. She was *that* tall. Her eyes were very large. Owl Eyes would have been a good nickname.

Her black hair reached her waist. She wore a silver dress that reached her ankles. Her necklace spelled the word *MONDAY*.

"Uh, er . . ." I stammered.

"We want to talk to you," Maria said. "We knocked on your front door. But nobody answered."

"So we were going to the back door," I said. "We, uh . . . got sidetracked."

"It's okay," LaMer said. "Come on." She led us to the front door. "What did you want to talk about?"

By now I'd recovered from my surprise. "We weren't snooping, Miss LaMer."

"No 'Miss.' Just call me 'LaMer.' Everybody does."

Just call me Cody. Everybody does. Maybe someday I could say that. But not now. LaMer's owl eyes jerked me out of my daydream.

"LaMer," I said. "Maria and I are detectives. We'd like to help you. Maybe we can find the crook that cheated you. Will you let us try?"

LaMer smiled. She seemed to have forgiven us for trespassing.

"How do you think you can help?" she asked.

"We can help look for the person who sold you the horse. But first we need to know more about carousel horses," I said. "And we need to know what the crook looked like."

"She was a woman," LaMer said. "A short, wide woman. She had gray hair that was as frizzy as a pot scrubber."

"Good description," I said. "We'll be watching for her."

"Cody used you for his current event today," Maria said. "Then Miss Reeding told us some carousel-horse history. But we need to know more. We need lots of facts."

"Please come inside," LaMer said. "You kids act more interested than the police did. I doubt that they're going to help. They say I was careless. And they're right."

"Please tell us all about it," I said. We followed her inside.

"I'm an artist," LaMer said. "A wood-carver. I also collect old carousel horses. So I combine these two interests. I repair old horses for customers. And I carve new horses for people who want them."

"Do many people buy carousel horses?" I asked.

"Yes," LaMer said. "They use them to decorate family or game rooms. Some business people want them too. Carousel horses attract people to restaurants or hotels."

"I saw one in a hotel lobby once," Maria said. "Could we see your collection?"

"Yes, indeed," LaMer said. "I like to show off my horses."

We followed her to the back of the house.

"You were looking into the log cabin," LaMer said. "My great grandfather built it during the frontier days. Before that, *his* father lived in a sod house. But it was ruined by rain."

"The front of the house looks newer," I said.

"My grandfather added it to the log cabin," LaMer said. "My father lived here. And now I live here. It's been in our family for years. It's a grand old home."

I wanted to ask about sod houses. But LaMer kept talking.

"The log cabin is my workshop," LaMer explained. She slipped off her shoes.

"I need to feel the sawdust on my toes," she said. "And the shavings. The spirit of the basswood speaks to my spirit. It guides my carving."

Maria and I stood speechless. We stared at LaMer. I inhaled the sharp smell of wood shavings. LaMer was one different lady. And her workshop was one different workshop.

Horse bodies hung from one wall. Unpainted horse legs hung from another wall. Tails hung there too. A horse's head lay unfinished on a worktable.

As we watched, LaMer picked up her mallet and a chisel. Tap. Tap. The horse's head took on more shape. It seemed like magic to me.

"Only a few people create and restore carousel horses," LaMer said. "I have carved 20 this year. And I have orders waiting to be made." She laid her mallet and chisel aside. "Look at this finished horse."

We looked. LaMer had mounted a black stallion on a brass pole. She had anchored the pole in a strong wooden box.

"This one's for my grandchildren," LaMer said. "They love sitting on it when they visit me. I'm going to add a music box too. They'll like that."

THE JAYHAWK HORSE MYSTERY

Maria laughed. "Some grandchildren have rocking horses. Yours have carousel horses. Cool!"

"Why does your necklace say *Monday*?" I asked.

"Because today is Monday," LaMer said. "It is, isn't it? Sometimes I forget what day it is. My necklaces remind me."

Maria nudged me. What sort of person didn't know what day it was? I wondered.

"LaMer," I said. "How did you know you were cheated? How could you tell the horse wasn't an antique?"

"Let me show you," LaMer said. "Here it is." She showed us the horse.

"I bought it in Kansas City," she told us.

"It looks old to me," I said.

LaMer lifted a strap on the saddle. "See?" She pointed to a small mark.

"What's that?" I asked. I saw the letter J and a picture of a hawk.

"It's a Kansas carver's trademark," LaMer said. "A jayhawk."

"Jayhawk's the nickname for University of Kansas students," Maria said.

"Yes," LaMer said. "That jayhawk is a mythical bird. But the word *jayhawk* meant something else in olden times. A long time ago, Kansas was a territory. It wasn't a state yet."

"Miss Reeding told us about that," I said. "Many people wanted Kansas to be a free state—no slavery. Others wanted it to enter the Union as a slave state."

"That's right," LaMer said. "Bands of horseback riders robbed slaveholders. They freed their slaves. People called those roughriders *Jayhawkers*."

"But how does the Jayhawk trademark tell you the horse isn't an antique?" I asked.

"Because the Jayhawk trademark is too modern," Maria pointed out.

"Right," LaMer said. "The mark was hidden under a saddle strap. I wish I had noticed it sooner. I wouldn't have bought the horse."

"Maybe we can find the crook," I said. "Maybe we can recover your money."

LaMer smiled. "Maybe," she said. "It won't hurt to try. Would you like to borrow this?" She held up a brightly colored book—*The Carousel Horse*.

"Yes," I said. "I'd really like to read it."

LaMer tucked it into my backpack. "Return it when you're finished, please."

"Will do," I promised. "Thanks a bunch."

Maria and I talked excitedly on the way home. We liked LaMer. And we wanted to learn more about carousel horses.

I really wanted to solve this mystery. I planned to spend the evening thinking about it.

Who could have bilked LaMer? Was that person really dangerous? Maybe all crooks were dangerous if cornered.

I tried not to think about that.

4

Stranger in the Night

I could hardly wait to get home. I grabbed the telephone book. In the yellow pages, I turned to *Antique Dealers.*

"Look, Maria," I said. "Cottonwood has two antique shops. Turkey Red Antiques and Pony Express Antiques. We'll need to visit both of them."

"Why?" Maria asked. "LaMer bought the fake horse in Kansas City. The crook wouldn't be hanging around Cottonwood."

"You're probably right," I said. "But we could ask some questions. Maybe antique dealers get together. Lots of them might know one another."

"Could be," Maria agreed. "Asking questions can't hurt. And it might help."

We changed clothes and went outside. Dark clouds had gathered in the sky. It looked like rain. So we went back inside.

"Let's work on our posters," Maria said. "Maybe we'll win the prize for our class." Maria cleared off the dining room table. "We can work here until supper time."

"I hope we win that field trip," I said. "Maybe we could go see those fossils Miss Reeding mentioned."

"We'll have to make a winning poster first," Maria said.

We each took a fresh sheet of paper. I wouldn't let Maria see my sheet. She wouldn't let me see her sheet. I drew some pictures. I could tell she was writing words.

Only slugs do drugs. I wrote the words on my paper. I liked the rhyme. People would remember a slogan that rhymed.

But what did a slug look like? I checked the dictionary. But I couldn't find a picture of a slug.

Just then, Mom arrived home from work. It was raining and she was wet. She snatched off her blond wig.

Mom's real hair lay flattened to her head. She called that her "peeled-onion" look. I liked her real hair best.

"Catch any shoplifters?" Maria asked.

"No," Mom said. "But I scared a couple from a bookstore."

"Too bad you didn't catch them," I said. "Maybe Maria and I can help you someday."

"Shopkeepers don't always want to catch shoplifters," Mom said. "They just want to stop them from stealing."

"Why is that?" Maria asked.

Mom sighed. "If they catch them, they should press charges. That means hiring a lawyer. That's expensive. They may have to go to court."

"That would take time away from their business," I said.

"Right," Mom agreed. "And it costs money. It's cheaper to hire a store detective. Knowing that detectives might be watching stops most shoplifters."

"But you'd nab a shoplifter if you saw a theft, right?" I asked.

"Right," Mom said. "I certainly would. That's my job."

COLUMBINE SCHOOL
Fort Morgan, CO

F Fra   +63886

Mom changed into jeans and a T-shirt. Then we all helped make supper. This was one of my favorite times. I liked it when the three of us worked together.

Maria set the table. I peeled potatoes. Mom fixed vegetables. And she made a huge omelet.

After supper, Maria worked on her poster. But I sat on the couch by the lamp. I wanted to read LaMer's book. I needed to know more about carousel horses.

I liked the smell of the slick paper and ink. I filled my lungs with it before I began to read.

Mom wanted to see the book too. She borrowed it for a minute. She looked at lots of the pictures. Then she returned it to me.

"Mom, did you know that lots of carousels were made in Kansas?" I asked.

"No," she said. "I didn't know that."

"In 1915, the Parker Company made one a week," I said. "And guess what?"

"What?" Maria asked. She was listening while she worked on her poster.

"President Eisenhower was a boy then," I said. "He worked for Mr. Parker. He sanded the horses before they were painted."

"Interesting," Mom said. "How about reading to yourself for a while?"

I took the hint. Mom was tired of listening. So I whispered to Maria. I had lots of facts to share.

"Every company had a master carver," I said. "They worked on the horse heads. That's the most important part of a horse. The other carvers worked on legs and tails."

"Cody," Maria said. "I need to think about my poster. I'll read the book later."

I sniffed. Mom! Maria! How could they ignore me like this? I sighed and read to myself.

The "king" horses made up the outer row of a carousel. Inner-row horses were smaller. And they weren't as brightly painted.

Right, I thought. I remembered racing Maria to the king horses. We sometimes rode the carousel in New York. I wondered if Maria remembered. But she was being uppity. I wasn't going to ask her now.

Reading made me sleepy. So did the sound of the rain. I decided to go to bed. I could read the book later. I took a warm shower. Then I crawled between the sheets.

I began to doze. Then I heard something. It sounded like singing. Yet there were no words. The sound came from outside.

Who would be singing in the rain? I crept from the bed and peered out the window.

At first I saw nothing but blackness. Rain left zigzaggy streaks on the windowpane.

Had I really heard singing? I wasn't sure. Then lightning lit the yard like a giant flashbulb. I gasped.

Someone was hugging our linden tree. The dark figure was singing. It was barefoot and wore a long hooded raincoat.

The lightning faded. Darkness covered the yard again.

"Mom!" I shouted. "Maria! Come here. Quick!"

They both came running. Mom snapped on the light.

"What's wrong?" Mom asked. "I thought you'd be asleep by now."

I told them about the stranger outside.

"Cody, you have one big imagination," Mom said. "There's nobody in our yard. Who would be singing? And who would be hugging the linden tree?"

I think Mom half believed me, though. She snapped off the light. Then we peered through the rain-streaked window. But we saw nothing. Maria sighed.

"Cody," Maria said. "You just had a nightmare. Go back to sleep."

I started to argue. But lightning flashed again. We all stared at the linden tree.

"See?" Mom said. "There's nobody there. You imagined it."

Mom and Maria left my room. But I knew I'd seen someone outside. Tomorrow I'd check for footprints.

5

A Very Bad Idea

The next morning nobody mentioned my imagination. I wanted to look for footprints. But I ate breakfast first.

Mom thought breakfast was magic. She thought it kept us safe all day.

Today Mom wore a fat black braid. It was a wig, of course. Her brown caftan reached her ankles.

Silver necklaces clanked when she moved. Her silver earrings jingled too. Just the noise might scare off shoplifters, I thought. I liked her quiet costumes best.

"Don't forget your poster, Cody," Maria said as we started for school. "Miss Reeding said we might have time to work on them in class."

She smiled at me. I liked that a lot. Maria's smiles made me feel special.

Once outside, I beelined to the linden tree. Maria laughed. But she followed me. We searched the ground carefully.

Grass grew right up to the tree trunk. It lay flat in some places. But wind and rain could have flattened it. I didn't want to think about what else might have flattened it.

"I don't see any footprints," Maria said. "You had a nightmare."

Maria was right. There weren't any footprints. But she was wrong about the nightmare. I saw someone hugging the linden. And I heard someone singing.

I remembered LaMer's bare feet in the sawdust. Had *she* been in our yard?

We were the last ones in the school building. The tardy bell buzzed like a wasp. We'd spent too much time looking for footprints.

A Very Bad Idea

"It's Miss Reeding's yellow day," Maria whispered.

I sighed. Who cared about clothes? But I did like Miss Reeding's jumper. Yellow made her look happy. But I didn't tell Maria that. I just slid into my seat.

"Today we'll work on the anti-drug posters," Miss Reeding said. "While you're working, be thinking of a class project. We have $100 from our car wash. We should use it soon."

"What kind of a project?" a boy called out. "What can we spend it on?"

"The project should be something that helps the community. It should also be fun," Miss Reeding said.

"Who gets to decide what we do?" a girl in the front of the room asked.

"We'll all present project ideas. Then we'll take a class vote," Miss Reeding said.

Suddenly I had a great project idea. I raised my hand. That's what you were supposed to do before you talked. But sometimes I forgot.

"Cody?" Miss Reeding said.

"We could buy a carousel horse," I said. "The Oregon Trail Nursing Home might like one. It's nice to do good things for old people."

Several kids laughed. Even Miss Reeding smiled.

"Why would a nursing home want a carousel horse?" she asked.

"LaMer made one for her grandchildren," I said. "She says they love to visit her. Most nursing home folks are grandparents. Grandchildren might visit more often if the home had a carousel horse."

"Cody!" Miss Reeding exclaimed. "That's really a fresh idea. It's new. It's different. Let's give it some thought."

"How much does a carousel horse cost?" a girl asked. She didn't raise her hand.

"Maybe the nursing home doesn't want a horse," a boy said. He didn't raise his hand, either. But Miss Reeding didn't yell at them. She was nice that way.

"I'll go to the nursing home," Miss Reeding said. "I'll mention Cody's idea to the director. Tomorrow I'll tell you what she says."

"I'll ask LaMer how much a horse costs," I said. "This could be a fun project."

"Fun for the home residents," Maria said. "And fun for the kids who visit."

We didn't get much done on our drug posters. We did too much talking. I peeked at Maria's paper. She had drawn an old house. Big deal.

What did a house have to do with drugs? I sighed. I still needed a picture of a slug. But I didn't know where to look. Maybe I could find another word to rhyme with *drug*.

A Very Bad Idea

The school day passed quickly. The dismissal bell rang. We ran out the door.

"Let's go to LaMer's house," I said. "We can ask the price of carousel horses."

"And about hugging our linden tree," Maria said. "Right?"

Maria read my mind again. How did she know I thought the linden hugger might be LaMer? I didn't admit she was right.

We knocked at LaMer's door. She let us in. Today her necklace said *TUESDAY*. She invited us to watch her work.

I liked the sharp smell of the basswood. And I noticed LaMer worked barefoot.

I didn't mention the linden tree—yet. Instead, I told her about needing a class project.

"How much do carousel horses cost?" I asked.

"Hand-carved ones are expensive," LaMer said. "Long ago, about 3,000 hand-carved horses existed. Less than 300 have survived.

"My prices begin at $1,300," she said. "And I only have a few antique horses to sell."

"Wow, $1,300!" I blurted out the words before I thought. I hadn't meant to sound so surprised.

LaMer smiled. "My top price is $4,000."

"Maybe we could buy a modern model," Maria said. "They're made of plastic, aren't they? Kids wouldn't know the difference."

"That's a possibility," LaMer said. "Even my modern basswood models are expensive."

I felt my face flush. I hoped I hadn't insulted LaMer. I wanted to change the subject—quickly. Maria helped me. She's good at smoothing over my mistakes.

"LaMer," Maria said. "Tell us about this horse." She pointed to a horse in the corner. "Why is one side brightly painted while the other side looks so bare?"

"Good question, Maria," LaMer said.

I felt my face cool down. I had wondered that too.

"In olden times, paint cost a lot," LaMer said. "So carousel owners only painted one side of the horses."

"How did they decide which side to paint?" Maria asked.

"Many people watched the carousels go around," LaMer said. "So owners painted the side the audience saw."

"That makes sense," I said.

"I've left my antique horses as they were," LaMer said. "Painting them would destroy their antique value."

She tapped her chisel. Basswood shavings dropped to the floor. I paid no attention to that. I wanted a polite way to ask about last night. Before I could say anything, LaMer spoke.

"I was in your yard last night, Cody," LaMer said.

"I must remember to talk to your mother about that."

I stood speechless. But again, Maria came to my rescue.

"Cody saw you," Maria said. "We thought he was dreaming, but . . ."

"What were you doing?" I asked.

"I was talking to the linden tree," LaMer said.

"Talking to a tree?" I asked. Mom wouldn't like hearing that. It was weird. Mom might tell us to stay clear of LaMer.

"My horses are made from basswood," LaMer said. "Basswood comes from linden trees. Yours is the only living linden in town."

"Oh," was all Maria said. Sometimes she lost her "smooth-over" ability. This was one of those times.

"I need to touch the linden now and then," LaMer said. "Its 'aliveness' inspires me. It helps me create. The renter before you let me come often. I hope your mother will too."

"Oh." I felt my world crashing. LaMer was weird. But I liked her. Mom worried about weirdness though. She might put LaMer off-limits for us.

Besides that, my classmates would laugh at me. My project idea had bombed big time. No class could afford a $1,300 horse! How could I face school tomorrow?

6

Barrel Boy

School happens—whether you're ready or not. I
wasn't ready. I spotted Miss Reeding. Today she wore
a blue jumper. It was blue Wednesday.

I kept out of her sight. I stayed on the soccer field
until the last bell rang. Then I slipped into my seat.

I hoped Miss Reeding wouldn't notice me. And I hoped the Oregon Trail Nursing Home didn't want a carousel horse. Maybe Miss Reeding wouldn't ask about horse prices.

She didn't—at least not right then.

"Good news, class," she said. "I talked to the nursing home director. She liked Cody's carousel-horse idea."

My heart dropped to my big toe. I wished she hadn't called it my idea—even if it had been. I'd be a laughingstock once the class found out about the cost.

But I was saved by the intercom.

"This is Mr. Sampson, YOUR PRINCIPAL," Wall Voice said.

For once, I welcomed his interruption. I didn't even mind his uppercase words.

"This is a Wednesday reminder," Wall Voice said. "Get to work on your posters. THE DEADLINE IS NEAR. Don't procrastinate."

I wondered what *procrastinate* meant. So did some other students. Miss Reeding asked Maria to look it up. That was good. It would kill some time.

But Maria worked fast. She found the word quickly.

"Procrastinate," she read. "To delay in doing a task."

Miss Reeding smiled. "We mustn't procrastinate," she said. "Let's finish those posters. Our English assignment can wait until tomorrow."

And that's what we did. I finally found a picture of a slug. I drew it with a black marker. *ONLY SLUGS DO DRUGS*. I printed the words in red. They looked important.

I was the first one to turn my poster in. My heart wasn't into making posters. I wanted to solve a mystery. I wanted to find the crook who cheated LaMer.

Now Maria let me see her poster. She had drawn an old house. Pills spilled from its door and windows. She had written four words at the bottom. *DRUGS? DON'T GO THERE!*

Miss Reeding smiled as she looked at it. She hadn't smiled when she looked at mine. But even I liked Maria's poster better than mine. Maybe her poster would win the field trip for us.

Miss Reeding told us to hurry. She collected all of our posters before we left for math class.

I knew I couldn't avoid telling the class my bad news forever. The end came Thursday morning. After Miss Reeding took roll, she asked me to tell the class what I'd learned from LaMer.

"The cheapest carousel horse is $1,300," I mumbled. I didn't look at anyone.

Nobody laughed. Instead, everyone groaned. I hated that too. So I tried to make things better.

"I'll talk to LaMer again," I told them. "Maybe she knows where we could get a cheaper horse."

So I headed to LaMer's after school. Maria went with me.

Today LaMer's black hair hung in a braid. That kept it out of the way while she carved.

I could almost taste the smell of fresh basswood. It left a sweet tartness on my tongue.

LaMer didn't know of any cheap horses. She only knew about expensive antique ones. So I changed the subject.

"LaMer," I said. "We still want to help you find Big Bilko."

"Big Bilko?" LaMer asked.

"The woman who cheated you," I said. "I nicknamed her."

LaMer laughed. "A good name. It fits."

"We're going to check out Cottonwood's antique shops," I said. "Big Bilko may be hiding out in one of them."

"No way, Cody," LaMer said. "I met her in Kansas City. She wouldn't risk coming to Cottonwood. She's probably headed for Chicago or New York."

"We'll check here just to be sure," I said. "Good detectives follow every lead."

LaMer just shook her head. She tap-tapped with

her mallet. Basswood shavings curled and dropped into the sawdust.

"Both of the local antique shops are owned by men," she said.

"Maybe they have wives," I said. "A wife could be an accomplice."

"I know the man at Turkey Red is married," LaMer said. "But I've never seen his wife. His shop features furniture.

"I don't know if the Pony Express owner is married. His shop features dishes." LaMer glanced at Cody. "Neither shop has carousel horses."

"The owners might not like kids in their shops," Maria said. "Some antiques are very fragile."

"We won't break anything," I said. "We'll be very careful."

I scowled at Maria. What was her problem? Didn't she want to check out the local shops?

"I'm going to do some investigating myself," LaMer said. "Next weekend."

"Where?" I asked. "Could Maria and I come with you?"

"I prefer to go alone," LaMer said. "But thanks for your offer. There's an art and antique show in Topeka. I'm planning to go next Saturday."

"You think Big Bilko might be there?" Maria asked.

"Probably not," LaMer said. "But I'm going to take a look."

"We'd better go now," I said. "Thank you for talking with us. If you hear of any cheap carousel horses, please let us know."

Maria and I headed toward downtown. We reached Turkey Red Antiques first. We stopped to case the place.

Junky furniture filled the shopwindow. There were rocking chairs, a bookcase, and an old desk. A spider had spun a web between two lamps. This looked like a shop where a crook might hide.

A man watched us through the dirty window. He had a barrel shape—short and stocky. Barrel Boy. The nickname popped into my mind.

Barrel Boy had squinty eyes. They were the color of gray flint. He stared at us. I felt like a bug under a microscope.

"Maybe we should come back later," Maria said.

"I'm not afraid," I said. I was afraid. But I wouldn't admit that to Maria.

I stepped inside the store first. Barrel Boy almost blocked the doorway. But I slipped in.

The shop smelled like the mice cage at school. We had one in the science room.

A huge fly zoomed past my left ear. Mom called them *bluebottles*. She always got a flyswatter and took care of them. Maybe Barrel Boy didn't have a flyswatter.

"What do you kids want?" he asked. "Do you have business here?"

Some greeting! He sure wasn't very friendly.

"My mom needs a new chair." I lied. Well, we could use a new chair, I reasoned. So it wasn't a total lie.

"I don't have any chairs," Barrel Boy said.

"What about those in the window?" Maria asked.

Barrel Boy's face flushed. "Do you kids have any money?" he asked.

I pulled a couple of crumpled dollar bills out of my pocket. Maria showed him four nickels. She'd already spent her allowance on cinnamon balls.

"That's not enough to buy a chair," Barrel Boy said. "Now get out of my shop. You have no business here. Leave before I call the cops."

"Mister," I said, "we just want to look around."

"I told you to get out," he said. "I mean it. Get. Right now."

I started to go. Barrel Boy could spell big trouble. But just then, Maria dropped a cinnamon ball. It rolled toward the back of the store.

I knew she had dropped it on purpose. We ran after it. Barrel Boy seemed too surprised to stop us.

The floor sloped toward the back door. The

cinnamon ball rolled under a desk. We chased it. It rolled under a sofa. We chased it. It rolled toward the basement steps.

Now Barrel Boy grabbed it. Drat. I wanted to see what was in that basement.

Maybe his wife was hiding out down there. Maybe she was Big Bilko. Now we'd never know for sure.

"Leave now!" Barrel Boy shouted.

He chased us. We ran for the front door. Once outside, we never looked back.

Would he chase us clear home? What if he caught us?

7

The Winner

Pain stabbed my left side. My lungs felt like hot sponges. I could hardly breathe. For a while, I heard Barrel Boy following us. Then the sound of his footsteps stopped.

But Maria and I kept running.

When we reached home, Mom called "hello." She was wearing her own blond hair—and her own jeans and shirt.

I almost forgot. This was her day off. Great. Now we'd have to explain.

"What's going on?" she asked.

Maria and I flopped onto the couch. It took awhile for us to catch our breath. That gave us some thinking time.

"We were racing home," I said. And that was pure truth.

"Cody won," Maria said.

"Hmmm," Mom said. She must have been short on curiosity today.

"I'm making pizza for supper," she said. "You two can help chop onions and olives."

And that's what we did. We chopped. We sliced. And we didn't say anything about visiting Turkey Red Antiques—or about Barrel Boy.

Pizza never tasted so good. After supper, Maria wrote in her secret journal. I tried to peek. But she sat so I couldn't see it. So I read the carousel-horse book.

After I went to bed, I watched outside. LaMer didn't come to hug the linden tree. Maybe it wasn't an every-night thing with her.

At school on Friday, I reported my findings. "LaMer doesn't know of any cheap carousel horses."

"Maybe we can buy something else for the home," one girl suggested.

"There's an art and antique show soon," I said. "We could look for something there. But it's in Topeka."

"Maybe our class could go," a boy said. "If we win the field trip."

"Then we could buy a gift for the nursing home at the fair," Maria said.

"Don't count your chickens before they're hatched," Miss Reeding said. "Let's come to order. It's time for English class."

Monday morning, Miss Reeding began reading a story to the class. I tried to pay attention. But I couldn't help thinking about LaMer's mystery.

Maria and I hadn't been able to visit the Pony Express Antiques store over the weekend. Mom had kept us busy. I was anxious to get back to my detective work.

Suddenly, Wall Voice interrupted Miss Reeding's

story. His voice exploded loudly over the intercom.

"ALL STUDENTS please report to the auditorium," he said. "We've chosen the WINNING POSTER. Please pass QUIETLY through the halls."

We were too excited to pass quietly. But we hurried to the auditorium.

We found our assigned seats. Everyone talked about posters and field trips—except me. I just listened. And breathed in the stale auditorium-air smell.

"Order, please," Wall Voice said.

A poster rested against the podium. We could only see the back of it. "Order, students! ORDER!"

Wall Voice didn't speak again until we sat quietly. Then he lifted the poster. He turned it toward us. *DRUGS? DON'T GO THERE!* I gasped. I heard Maria gasp.

"The winner of the poster contest is Maria Romero," Wall Voice said. "Miss Reeding's sixth-grade homeroom WINS THE FIELD TRIP."

Wall Voice said more. But nobody listened. Everyone clapped and whistled. Finally, Miss Reeding led us back to our classroom.

I felt numb. I had wanted to win—even though I knew Maria's poster was better.

Now Maria would be famous—for a while. Everyone crowded around her. Everyone congratulated her.

I didn't say anything to her. I was totally jealous. I couldn't help it. And I felt rotten about it.

"Maybe we can take that field trip to Topeka," a boy called out.

We talked about that for a while. Everyone wanted to go. We voted for it.

"I'll ask Mr. Sampson to okay the Topeka-art-show trip," Miss Reeding said. "It will be educational. And it will be fun."

"Maybe there'll be carousel horses for sale there," a girl called out. "LaMer's not the only one with carousel horses."

"We'll see," Miss Reeding said. "The show is Saturday. We don't have long to prepare. I'm not promising you anything."

"LaMer's going to that show," I said. Everyone looked at me. Now I had the limelight again. I felt a little better. "Maybe she could go with us."

"We'll see," Miss Reeding said. "Now let's get back to English class. Open your books to page 36."

Somehow the school day ended. I walked home with Maria as usual. She said nothing. I said nothing.

My neck itched. Sometimes I itched when I was about to tell a lie.

"I'm glad your poster won, Maria," I said. I scratched my neck.

"Thanks, Cody," Maria said. "I know you wanted to win too. But there'll be another time. This wasn't the last contest in the world."

Maria smiled at me. And I felt special again—almost.

Then she offered me a cinnamon ball. I took it. It was her way of trying to make me feel better. And it did. The hotness in my mouth made the rest of me feel cool.

"Your poster was best," I said. And my neck didn't itch. "You deserved to win. I'm jealous. But I'll get over it. And you know what?"

"No," Maria said. "What?"

"I have another plan for being famous," I said. "You're the very first person I've told. But someday I'm going to get my picture on a postage stamp."

"Cool!" Maria said. "Maybe I can help. What do we have to do?"

"I'm not sure yet," I admitted. "But I'll find out."

"In the meantime, let's think about the field trip," Maria said.

"Okay." I thought she'd be more excited about the postage stamp thing. I wondered if she was a little jealous of me too.

Maybe I could get us both on the same stamp. We could be detective partners. Would the post office go for that? I'd have to find out.

"Maybe Big Bilko will be at Topeka," Maria said. "But how would we find her?"

"LaMer gave us her description," I said. "First, we'll look for people selling carousel horses. Then we'll look for someone matching her description. Finding her might be dangerous. We may need help to capture her."

"Right," Maria agreed. "Lots of help." She sighed. "Cody, we're talking as if this trip's a sure thing. Let's just cool our jets until tomorrow."

That night at supper, we told Mom the news about Maria's poster. We also told her about the field trip. And we mentioned that we might need an adult chaperone.

"Don't count on me," she said. "I have to work Saturday."

That didn't worry me. I figured LaMer would want to chaperone us.

After supper, Maria opened her secret journal. "Want to see some of my story ideas?" she asked.

At first I couldn't believe it. She was going to let me look. Then I knew why. She still wanted to make me feel better about losing the contest. Maria's a great friend.

"Sure," I said. "What have you been writing?"

She held the notebook toward me. I saw a bunch of questions. I read the list out loud.

> How come wrong numbers are
> never busy?
>
> What do you pack styrofoam in?
>
> Would the ocean be deeper if
> sponges didn't live there?
>
> Does war determine who's right?
> Or who's left?

I smiled at Maria. I didn't tell her I thought her questions were crazy. "Where are you going to find the answers?" I asked.

"Don't know," Maria said. "Maybe you can help me."

I knew Maria was just being polite. She wanted to find the answers herself. I closed her notebook and gave it back to her.

Right now I wanted to think about LaMer—and Big Bilko. Would we be able to catch this crook?

8

A Change of Plans

Tuesday morning we left for school early. We had a plan. Mom left earlier than we did. So we didn't have to explain.

"Let's be careful," Maria said. She put her headphones in her backpack. "Maybe the owner of Pony Express Antiques hates kids too."

A Change of Plans

"We'll smile a lot," I said. "That usually helps. LaMer said the shop used to be a mail stop. You know, for the old Pony Express riders."

Maria ignored me. She wasn't really into history.

Pony Express Antiques looked nothing like Turkey Red Antiques. It looked clean. The windows sparkled. Bright carpet covered the floor.

LaMer was right about the dishes. We saw hundreds of them. There was lots of crystal and china.

I don't know much about fancy dishes. But the shop made me want to hold my breath. I moved slowly and carefully.

"I guess the carpet protects the dishes," Maria said. "If they're dropped, I mean."

She held her breath too—for a while. But you can't do that forever.

"May I help you?" a young woman asked. She wore pink ballet slippers and walked on tiptoes. Was she practicing for a dance recital? She also wore a pink leotard.

I wondered if she knew about Mr. Leotard. He invented leotards in Paris years ago. Now he's an eponym.

Maria spoke up before I could ask.

"We need to see the shop owner," Maria said.

"He doesn't arrive until noon," Ballet Slippers said. "Maybe I could help you find something."

"We're interested in carousel horses," Maria said. She offered Ballet Slippers a cinnamon ball. But she didn't want one.

"We had a carousel horse last week," Ballet Slippers said. "But the boss sold it quickly. He prefers dishes."

"Do you remember who bought it?" I asked. "Our friend, LaMer . . ."

"LaMer didn't buy it," Ballet Slippers said. "The buyer was a stranger."

"You'd never seen her before?" I asked.

"That's right. And I know everyone in Cottonwood. The buyer bought the horse to resell for profit. I told my boss we should have asked more for it."

"What did he say?" Maria asked.

"He said he didn't care," Ballet Slippers said. "He only likes dishes. He took that horse in trade for some cut glass. He was glad to get rid of it."

"What did the woman look like?" I asked.

Ballet Slippers thought for a moment. "She was short. And wide. And she had frizzy gray hair."

"Big Bilko!" I said.

Maria nodded. "Could be," she said.

"The woman paid cash," Ballet Slippers said. "So I don't know her name."

"What did the horse look like?" I asked.

"It was old," Ballet Slippers said. "It was brightly painted on the right side. But it had hardly any paint on the left side. And it had three white daisies painted near the tail."

"Where was she going to resell the horse?" Maria asked.

"She didn't say," Ballet Slippers said. "But she mentioned something about an art show soon."

I had more questions. But Maria pointed to the clock.

"Cody, we're going to be late," she said. "Let's go."

Sometimes Maria was so bossy. But she was usually right. We hurried from the shop.

"That resell lady might be Big Bilko," I said. "Maybe she'll raise the price and cheat someone else."

"She can set her own price," Maria said. "There's nothing illegal about that. But she shouldn't lie about the horse's age."

"Maybe she'll be in Topeka this weekend," I said.

"And maybe we'd better run," Maria said. "I just heard the warning bell."

We sprinted, but we didn't make it. The tardy bell rang as we hurried down the hall.

It's a rotten feeling to be late to school. Everyone stared as we walked into the room. Two boys laughed. My face had a sunburn-on-the-inside feeling. I thought Miss Reeding would send us to the office.

She didn't need to. Wall Voice stood right there in our room. He glared at us until we sat down. We sat very quickly.

"Now, students," Wall Voice began. "I hope you appreciate this opportunity. I don't allow field trips every day. They are special events. VERY SPECIAL."

"We appreciate that," Miss Reeding said.

"You are fortunate that LaMer will help chaperone," Wall Voice said.

Maria and I smiled at each other. We hadn't known that LaMer had agreed to chaperone. This promised to be a great trip.

LaMer could identify Big Bilko if Maria and I spotted her. Big Bilko might be in disguise. But LaMer would recognize her. Besides, it's hard to disguise short and wide.

"BUT REMEMBER . . ." Wall Voice continued.

Did Wall Voice know that he talked in uppercase? I wondered.

". . . that you represent Chisholm Trail Middle School." Wall Voice looked serious. "People will notice your behavior. SET A GOOD EXAMPLE FOR OTHERS. Bring back ideas with educational value. OBEY MISS REEDING. And most of all . . ."

He hesitated. We waited, expecting the worst.

". . . HAVE FUN!" he finished.

Maybe Wall Voice was okay after all. But I breathed

easier after he left the room. Miss Reeding said nothing about our being late.

"Okay, students," Miss Reeding said. "The bus leaves promptly at 8:00 on Saturday morning. Be here. You can sit where you want—as long as you behave."

She held up a red and white booklet. "I have a brochure about the show."

"Read it to us," someone called.

"What will we see?" another voice called.

"Do we need lunch money?" a third voice asked.

"Show admission is free," Miss Reeding said. "You can bring your own lunch. Or your can bring money to buy lunch there. It will take an hour to get there. We'll return about 4:00."

"Does anyone advertise carousel horses?" I asked.

"Yes," Miss Reeding said. "Three vendors list carousel horses. We'll check them out. Maybe we'll find one we can afford."

And maybe Big Bilko will be there, I thought. We could buy a horse. And we could catch a crook. Most importantly, maybe we could prove ourselves in Cottonwood as detectives.

Just before lunch, Wall Voice returned. Suddenly the room was so quiet you could hear a pin drop.

"I have good news," he said. "And I have bad news."

Don't be corny, I thought. But he caught our attention and we listened.

"The bad news is that LaMer just called me. She can't go with us on Saturday."

Everyone groaned—especially Maria and me. We needed LaMer with us.

"The good news is . . ." Wall Voice paused. "I'M GOING IN HER PLACE."

Pin-drop silence fell again. Nobody wanted Wall Voice on this trip!

Then Maria began clapping. Maria the peacemaker. Miss Reeding began clapping too. And I joined in—reluctantly. Soon the whole class clapped. And Wall Voice smiled.

It promised to be some trip.

9

The Art Fair

After school, Maria and I knocked on LaMer's door. We smelled the sharp fragrance of basswood. She even had a wood shaving caught in her long hair.

She still wore her Monday necklace. Should we tell her it was Tuesday? I didn't tell her. Neither did Maria.

"Come in, kids. What's going on?"

"That's what we want to know," Maria said. "First you were going on the field trip. Then you backed out. What happened?"

"We were counting on you," I said. "We're going to look for Big Bilko. She may have even been in Cottonwood last week."

"Why do you say that?" LaMer asked.

We told LaMer about Ballet Slippers at Pony Express Antiques.

"A customer bought a carousel horse," Maria said.

"She said she planned to resell it," I added. "She might be at the art fair on Saturday. Please come with us."

"I can't," LaMer said. "I've ordered special blocks of basswood. They're going to arrive on Saturday. I have to be home to receive them."

"Wall Voice is going in your place," I said.

"Who?" LaMer asked.

"Mr. Sampson, the principal," Maria said. "We'd rather have you."

"We think Big Bilko may be at the fair," I said. "It's our chance to do some detective work. Maybe we can nab her. Maybe you could get your money back."

"I'd like to see her arrested," LaMer said. "I want my money, of course. But as long as she's free, she can cheat others too. I don't like that."

"So we'll help catch her," I said.

"She could be dangerous," LaMer said. "You'd better forget about her. Just have fun. Enjoy the art show."

"But . . . but . . ." I spluttered.

"No more 'buts,' " LaMer said. "Stop by here when you get back. You can tell me all about the show. I really wish I could go."

We left LaMer and trudged home.

"We're still going to look for Big Bilko, aren't we?" Maria asked. "I'm not afraid."

"Sure," I said. "We'll look. We'll find her if she's there. But let's keep it our secret until it happens."

On Saturday morning, Mom made us eat breakfast. We weren't hungry. But we ate anyway. Mom had a thing about breakfast.

Mom gave us money for lunch and souvenirs. Finally, we headed for school.

We could see the yellow bus a block away. I smelled the diesel exhaust. Yuck. I didn't want that smell in my lungs. But a guy had to breathe.

Miss Reeding wore her red jumper—her Monday color. But it was Saturday. Would this throw off her whole week's dress schedule?

Wall Voice arrived. He wore jeans and a T-shirt. He also wore a blue athlete's jacket. It had a red jayhawk on the back. He looked like a real person.

However, he used his principal's voice to call roll. Everyone answered. Then we boarded the bus.

"Students," he said. "Today I'm your bus driver. I'm also your chaperone. Please choose partners. STICK WITH YOUR PARTNER ALL DAY. Each of you is responsible for your partner's well-being."

Of course Maria and I chose each other.

"Either Miss Reeding or I will be at the bus," Wall Voice said. "Every team of partners will report to us each hour. This is to guarantee your safety."

He plopped onto the driver's seat. The bus door gave a *whoosh*. And the gears ground into action. We were off! My heart leaped.

Kids yelled questions to Wall Voice.

"Were you a football player in college?" one boy asked.

"No," Wall Voice said. "I never played football."

"Basketball?" a girl called out.

"No," Wall Voice said. "I never played basketball."

"What sport did you play?" the first boy asked.

Just then a semi-truck passed us. We couldn't hear Wall Voice's answer. And nobody asked again. We just talked and laughed and talked some more.

"Look!" Maria shouted. She pointed to Topeka's

gold capitol dome. She's good at being the first one to see stuff. The dome glinted in the sunlight.

Miss Reeding told us about a mural inside the capitol. "Kansas artist John Stuart Curry painted it," she said. "The mural shows John Brown. He fought hard against slavery in Kansas.

"The mural also shows three small skunks," she said. "They represent the legislators. As you can imagine, the legislators were slow to pay Curry for his mural."

I laughed. So did Maria.

Wall Voice drove to a large field. An entry-gate sign said *ART FAIR*.

A security guard met us in the parking lot. He boarded our bus.

"Welcome to the art fair," he said. "I'm Sergeant Watchal. I'm here to keep you and your bus safe. Remember where your bus is. Come to me if you have any problems."

Maria and I followed Miss Reeding off the bus. Hundreds of booths dotted the fairgrounds. Blue. Green. Yellow. It looked like a colorful flower garden.

We threaded our way through the crowds to the exhibits. Freedom! We were on our own for an hour.

The first thing we noticed was the food. I loved the smell of hot dogs. Pink cotton candy tempted Maria.

But we decided not to buy anything yet. We had some snooping to do first.

Many vendors had tents behind their booths. They had slept here. I wished we could see inside the tents. But tent flaps covered the openings.

There were many different kinds of art. We saw oil and watercolor paintings. A wood-carver chipped at a replica of an elephant. A jeweler strung necklaces of shiny beads.

We also saw pottery exhibits. One potter slapped gray clay onto her wheel. We watched her shape it into a mug.

We looked for antique exhibits. There were lots of those. At last we found one with a carousel horse. The owner told us about his horse.

"It's a Philadelphia-style horse," he said. "Collectors consider this style very elegant."

"It's not very brightly colored," Maria said.

"That's part of its style," the man said. "The Philadelphians used dull colors. They were very realistic."

"How much does it cost?" I asked.

"The price on this one is $1,000," he said.

We didn't hang around that booth very long. The horse didn't match Ballet Slipper's description. It hadn't come from Pony Express Antiques in Cottonwood. Besides, our class couldn't afford it.

"Oh, Cody," Maria said as we walked on. "Look at this booth. I wonder if LaMer has a horse like this one."

I stared. "Wow!" I said. "It looks like a jewelry exhibit."

The vendor smiled at us. "That's a Coney Island-type horse," he said. "It's very old. These horses were fancy in design. But the jewels were just glass."

"How much is it?" Maria asked.

"Twenty-five," the vendor said.

Maria and I looked at each other. Here was a horse we could afford. And a pretty one too.

"Our class has $25," I said. "We'll get our teacher. She'll want to see this horse."

The dealer laughed. "It's 25 *hundred* dollars, sonny. Nobody's selling a horse like this for 25 dollars."

"We knew that," Maria said. She tried to cover my mistake. But the dealer kept laughing. We hurried away.

We reported to the bus on the hour. Then we bought cotton candy. And we continued our search for carousel horses—and Big Bilko.

We reached another antique booth. And there was the horse Ballet Slippers had described. It looked old. It had bright paint on one side. And three daisies were painted near the tail.

I nudged Maria. We inched closer to the booth. A thin man sat beside the cash box. The tent flap behind him was closed. We couldn't see inside.

Maria and I whispered our plans.

"I'm going to talk to this guy." I said.

"But a man's running the booth," Maria said. "I don't think we'll find Big Bilko here."

"She could be inside the tent," I replied.

"Be careful," Maria said. "He hasn't done anything wrong. There's no law against reselling an antique."

"I'm just going to talk to him," I said. "But be ready to run for help. We're responsible for each other, you know."

I tried to sound brave. I tried to sound sure of myself. But I knew I didn't fool Maria. We were both scared of what might happen next.

10

The Chase

    I approached the man in the antique booth. He wore bib overalls and a frayed straw hat. A dirty-looking toothpick hung from his mouth. I nicknamed him *Toothpick*.

Maria stood to one side. We were partners—a team. And we were alert to danger.

"Mister," I said. "I like your merry-go-round horse." I played dumb. I didn't call it a carousel horse. "Where did you get it?"

"That's for me to know," he said, sneering. "And for you to find out. Antique dealers don't blab about where they got stuff."

"I'm sorry I asked," I said. My neck itched a little. "How much does it cost?"

"More money than you've got, kid," he said. "Unless, of course, you've got $3,000 cash." He wiggled his toothpick. It almost fell out of his mouth.

"I don't have that much cash with me," I admitted. "How old is this horse? It looks very old."

"It's an oldie all right," he said. His voice had an oily sound. He gave me a sly wink. "I found it on my last buying trip to England."

"Across the ocean?" I asked. "That England?"

"That's the one," Toothpick said. "Why, royalty may have ridden on this horse. Maybe old King George rode it. Even the queen mother may have sat on it."

I saw Maria trying to peek inside the tent. But she had no luck. The flap blocked her view.

Maybe I was wrong about this horse. Maybe lots of them had daisies near their tails. I thought of more questions. I wanted to keep Toothpick talking.

"The left side of your horse hardly has any paint on it," I said. "I'd want a horse painted on both sides." I was testing him. Did he know why one side was almost bare?

"Paint used to be very expensive," he said. "Owners couldn't afford to paint both sides."

This guy knew his stuff. I tried to think of something else to ask. I couldn't just ask if he had cheated LaMer.

Besides, a woman had cheated LaMer in Kansas City. Not a man.

Then I remembered something important. Wow! I had an awesome idea. But it could be dangerous. We had to be careful.

"Well, thanks for the information," I told Toothpick and walked away.

I pulled Maria aside. We talked softly and made our plans. We wanted to trap this guy.

"I'll stay here," Maria said. "I'll stand where he won't notice me. I'll follow him if he leaves."

"Good," I said. "And watch for Big Bilko. She may be in hiding nearby."

"Talk to Sergeant Watchal," Maria said. "See what he thinks."

I poked along until I was out of Toothpick's sight. Then I sprinted to the parking lot. Sergeant Watchal stood talking to Wall Voice. I knew it was rude, but I interrupted them.

"I need to talk with you, Sergeant Watchal," I said.

"What is it, Cody?" Wall Voice asked. "Don't be bothering the sergeant."

Sergeant Watchal stepped toward me. "Do you have a problem, Cody?"

"I think I've discovered a thief, sir," I said.

"Cody!" Wall Voice scolded again. But Sergeant Watchal drew me aside.

"Suppose you tell me about it, Cody," he said.

I whispered my thoughts in Sergeant Watchal's ear. Wall Voice's face grew red. But he didn't try to stop me again. Sergeant Watchal listened carefully. Then he nodded.

"We'd better have a talk with this man," Sergeant Watchal said. We walked to the antique booth. Wall Voice followed us. Maria stood to one side keeping watch.

Toothpick squirmed when he saw Sergeant Watchal. He looked like he might run.

"May I see your vendor's license, please?" Sergeant Watchal asked.

Toothpick stalled a long time. He looked in his shirt pocket. He looked in his cash box. He looked in his overalls pocket. Then he found the license stuck in his hatband.

My heart took a dive. He had a license. Maybe I had been wrong about him.

"Tell me about this horse," Sergeant Watchal said.

Toothpick repeated his "I-found-it-in-England" lie.

"Sir," Sergeant Watchal said. "This boy has something to say. Go ahead, Cody. Speak up."

"Mister," I began. "In England, carousel horses turn clockwise. I read that in LaMer's book."

"Who's LaMer?" Toothpick asked.

"Don't interrupt him," Sergeant Watchal said.

"This horse didn't come from England," I said. "An English horse would be brightly painted on the left side. That's the side an English audience would see. This horse is bright on the right side. I think you're lying."

Just then the tent flap opened. Big Bilko appeared. I recognized her from LaMer's description.

"What's going on out here?" she shouted. "We paid for this space. We have our rights."

Her shouting distracted Sergeant Watchal. The sergeant turned to look at Big Bilko. And Toothpick ran—fast.

Now what? If Sergeant Watchal chased Toothpick, Big Bilko might escape. If he didn't, Toothpick would escape.

"Stop that man," Sergeant Watchal shouted. "He has some explaining to do." Sergeant Watchal moved closer to Big Bilko.

To my surprise, Wall Voice chased Toothpick. He

caught him before he'd gone 100 yards. He made the capture look easy.

He brought Toothpick back in a hurry. Wow! Wall Voice wasn't even panting for breath.

"Should I make a citizen's arrest?" Wall Voice asked.

"I'll take care of him," Sergeant Watchal said. He pulled out handcuffs. By now a crowd had gathered.

"Put the cuffs away," Toothpick said. "We'll come quietly."

Then I noticed LaMer standing in the crowd. My mouth dropped open in surprise.

Things moved quickly after that. LaMer told us her basswood delivery had arrived early. So she decided to come to the art fair after all.

Sergeant Watchal explained what had happened. Then LaMer identified Big Bilko. It turned out that Toothpick was Big Bilko's husband. They worked together in their scam.

They promised to return LaMer's money. And they said she could keep the horse with the Jayhawk trademark.

Reporters arrived and snapped our pictures. Sergeant Watchal put Toothpick and Big Bilko into a squad car. They drove away. The excitement died down after that.

LaMer smiled at us. "You two are good detectives," she said. "You really used your head, Cody."

"Thanks," I said, blushing.

"I also have a surprise for you," she said.

"What?" I asked.

"I'm going to give your class the Jayhawk horse," she said. "You can donate it to the Oregon Trail Nursing Home."

"Awesome!" I shouted.

"I'll mount a music box in it too," LaMer said. "I like to do things for my community. Cottonwood's a good place to live."

Maria and I felt proud. I might not be famous. But I'd helped solve the case of the carousel horse. I'd done something worthwhile.

We told LaMer she could hug our linden tree anytime.

Wall Voice and Miss Reeding herded everyone back to the bus. They decided we'd all had enough excitement for one day.

On the bus, a boy called out to Wall Voice. "Wow! You can really run!"

Wall Voice grinned into the rearview mirror. "I told you I excelled in track and field."

Track and field! Those were the words we hadn't heard on the bus. He'd been a runner. From now on, I'd forget about calling him Wall Voice.

Mr. Sampson was one great principal. He was one okay guy too. He might even have some good advice for me. Maybe *he* knew how I could get my picture on a postage stamp.

No, I'm not famous yet. But there's always tomorrow.

COLUMBINE SCHOOL
Fort Morgan, CO